HOW LLAMA SAVED THE DAY

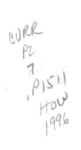

First-Start® Legends

HOW LLAMA SAVED THE DAY

A STORY FROM PERU

Retold by Janet Palazzo-Craig
Illustrated by Charles Reasoner

Troll

Long ago, there lived a farmer and his family. Their greatest treasure was their llama. For the llama carried heavy loads back and forth from the fields.

The farmer always took good care of the llama. One day, he took it to a special place where the grass was green and tender. "Eat, my llama," said the farmer. But the llama would not eat.

The next three days, the same thing happened. "Llama, you must eat," said the farmer. "If you do not, you will die."

Instead of eating, the llama began to cry. Big tears rolled down its face.

To the farmer's surprise, the llama spoke. "A terrible thing is going to happen. The sea will flood the land. Everyone will die."

"How can we save ourselves?" the farmer asked.

"Go to the highest mountain," said the llama. "There you will be safe."

The man ran home. "Stop
everything!" he cried. "We must
go. A great flood is coming! Our
llama said so."

"Have you been out in the sun
too long?" said his wife, who had
never heard of a talking llama.

13

But soon the man convinced her.
They packed and set off.

After a time, they came upon two
guanacos. "Follow us up the mountain,
or you will die in the flood," said the
llama. The animals followed.

Next, they came upon some flamingos. The llama told them what to do. Away they flew to the mountain.

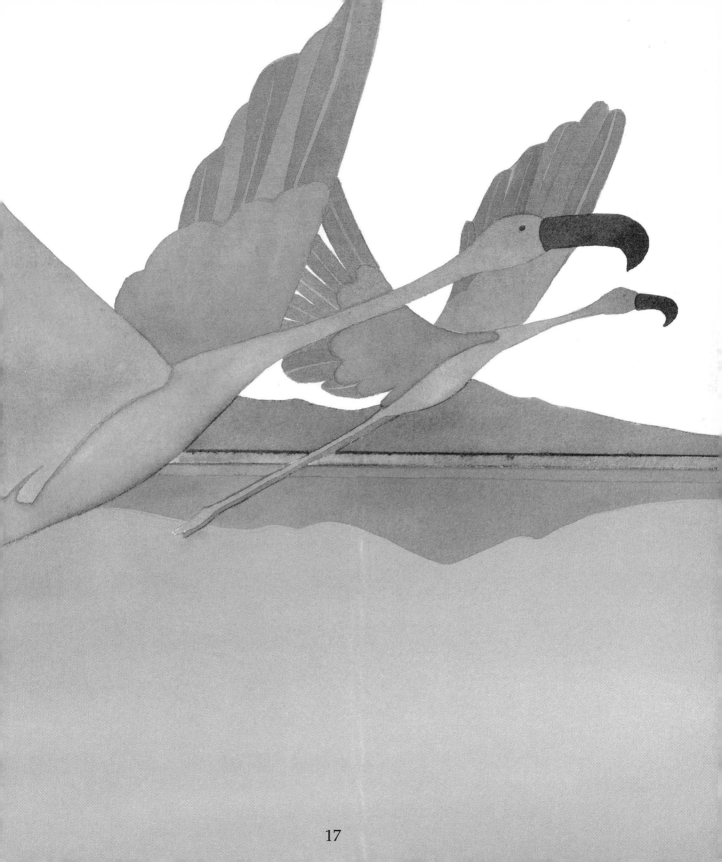

The climbers were tired, but they saw the waters rising behind them. They hurried along.

They came to a puma and her cubs. The llama warned them. They, too, joined the group.

Farther along, two chinchillas were resting. "If you don't want to drown, follow us!" said the llama. And they did.

On a rocky ledge, they met
three condors. When the birds
heard of the flood, they flew to
the mountain.

A family of foxes came to find out what was happening. "Beware the flood," said the llama. But the foxes did not believe the llama. They did not follow.

So it went that the llama told all they met about the flood. At last, the group reached the mountaintop. And just in time—below them the flood waters were high.

"Look," cried the farmer. The foxes were hurrying up the mountain to escape the water! They made it, but there was very little room, and their tails hung into the water.

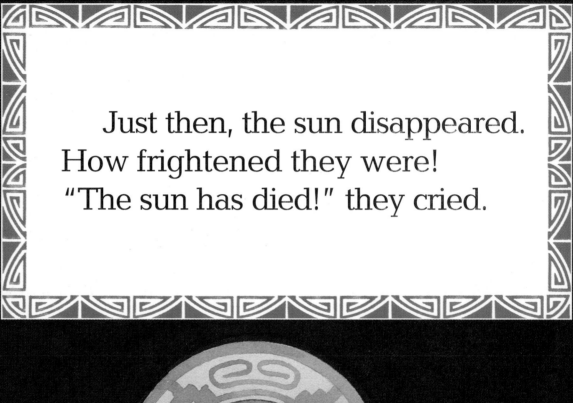

Just then, the sun disappeared.
How frightened they were!
"The sun has died!" they cried.

"Do not fear," said the llama. Suddenly, the waters stopped rising. The sky grew bright.

"The sun was resting," said the llama. "From now on, the sun will shine for us in the day. At night, the moon will come to show us her beauty."

When the waters went down, the family and the animals returned to their homes. The first to climb down were the foxes. They had been saved, but they now had black tips on the ends of their tails. That was where the dark waters had touched them.

Today, the people remember the story of the talking llama. To give thanks, they put bells and ribbons on their llamas. They take the llamas to eat tender, green grass. As the animals eat, the people play their flutes. The llamas move their ears in time to the music—but not one of them has ever talked again!

How Llama Saved the Day is a legend from Peru. It takes place in the Andes Mountains, which lie east of the Pacific Ocean. This legend is similar to other stories about floods—for example, the story of Noah and the ark. Such tales of enormous floods can be found throughout the world among many different cultures.

"antara"
(panflute)